GET A CLUE

THE CURSE OF THE CROSSBOW ARCHER

A PICTURE MYSTERY

GET A CLUE

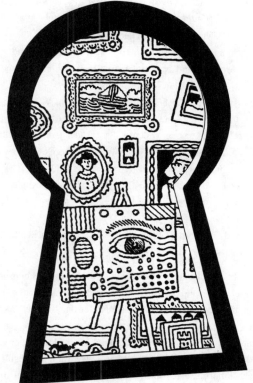

THE CURSE OF THE CROSSBOW ARCHER

A PICTURE MYSTERY

Julian Press

GROSSET & DUNLAP

GROSSET & DUNLAP
Published by the Penguin Group
Penguin Group (USA) Inc., 375 Hudson Street, New York, New York 10014, USA
Penguin Group (Canada), 90 Eglinton Avenue East, Suite 700, Toronto, Ontario M4P 2Y3, Canada
(a division of Pearson Penguin Canada Inc.)
Penguin Books Ltd., 80 Strand, London WC2R 0RL, England
Penguin Group Ireland, 25 St. Stephen's Green, Dublin 2, Ireland
(a division of Penguin Books Ltd.)
Penguin Group (Australia), 250 Camberwell Road, Camberwell, Victoria 3124, Australia
(a division of Pearson Australia Group Pty. Ltd.)
Penguin Books India Pvt. Ltd., 11 Community Centre, Panchsheel Park, New Delhi—110 017, India
Penguin Group (NZ), 67 Apollo Drive, Rosedale, North Shore 0632, New Zealand
(a division of Pearson New Zealand Ltd.)
Penguin Books (South Africa) (Pty.) Ltd., 24 Sturdee Avenue,
Rosebank, Johannesburg 2196, South Africa

Penguin Books Ltd., Registered Offices: 80 Strand, London WC2R 0RL, England

Copyright © 2006 by cbj Verlag, a division of Verlagsgrupped Random House GmbH, Munchen, Germany.
Translated and adapted by the Miller Literary Agency, LLC. All rights reserved.
Cover background copyright © Mayang Murni Adnin, 2001-2006.
Published by Grosset & Dunlap in 2008, a division of Penguin Young Readers Group,
345 Hudson Street, New York, New York 10014.
GROSSET & DUNLAP is a trademark of Penguin Group (USA) Inc.
Printed in the U.S.A.

Library of Congress Control Number: 2008005233

ISBN 978-0-448-44876-3   10 9 8 7 6 5 4 3 2 1

INTRODUCTION

The Sugar Shack sold the best candy in Hillsdale, the tiny town where best friends Josh, David, and Lily lived. The Sugar Shack was owned by Lily Shipman's uncle, Frank. Lily, David, and Josh spent a lot of time there after school. Sometimes Lily's other uncle, Tony, dropped by. Tony was a police detective and a sucker for lollipops. The three friends loved mysteries, suspense stories, and solving puzzles, so they constantly harassed Tony with questions about his work. One day Tony suggested they start up their own detective agency. They could use the candy storage room in the attic of the Sugar Shack as their headquarters, and Frank and Tony could be their technical consultants. The three friends jumped at the chance! It was no time at all before they solved their very first case . . .

MEET THE DETECTIVES

 Lily Shipman is extremely athletic. She's fast and competitive. She loves a good challenge.

 Inspector Tony Shipman is a night owl. When the rest of the world is asleep, he's always hard at work at his computer, solving cases.

 David Doyle has a sensitive ear, especially for birdcalls. The clucking of his loyal cockatoo, Robinson, is like a second language to him.

 Frank Shipman, the owner of the Sugar Shack, is like some of the chocolates he sells: tough on the outside, gooey on the inside.

 Josh Rigby has eagle eyes and loves gadgets. His pockets are always full of tools to use in unexpected situations.

 Robinson, David's beloved cockatoo, is an expert at following suspects. The element of surprise works in his favor: No one expects a bird to be a detective!

You can help Lily, David, and Josh solve the mysteries in this book. Just read the stories, and try to answer the questions. Here's a hint: Look at the pictures for clues!

CLUE ONE: A Bad Start

"Before we begin, I'd like to offer my sincerest condolences," said Alfred Elmira, attorney-at-law. He was welcoming Dr. Amelia Horton's closest friends and family to the reading of Amelia's will.

Mr. Elmira was Frank Shipman's close friend, and had invited Lily, David, and Josh to the reading to observe the proceedings.

Amelia's family gathered around the portrait of her on the wall, waiting for Mr. Elmira to continue.

Mr. Elmira went on. "Despite the fact that I asked you here today for the reading of the last will and testament of the late Dr. Horton, we cannot proceed for one simple reason: We haven't found it yet!"

Everyone gasped. Horton's relatives' faces revealed a combination of disappointment and anger.

"But don't worry. We will do everything we can to keep you updated on the situation."

Mr. Elmira's reassurances didn't seem to satisfy the group: Everyone was grumbling.

"I know someone who has already gotten her part of the inheritance," Lily remarked to her friends.

"Do you think it was a gift from Dr. Horton?" asked Josh, already catching on to what Lily meant.

"It had better be, because if it's a theft, it's not very discreet . . ."

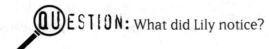 **QUESTION:** What did Lily notice?

CLUE TWO: A Weird Will

Lily spotted the big brooch Amelia Horton was wearing in her portrait on the dress of the woman in black! The woman in black introduced herself to Mr. Elmira as Rita Hartford, but the detectives couldn't figure out what her relation was to the deceased.

The attorney continued his speech.

"Ladies and gentlemen, please, be calm. I assure you, I brought you here for a reason. I have an envelope to give to each of you from Dr. Horton!"

Alfred Elmira led the group into another room and invited them to sit around a table. The attorney took out the envelopes from his briefcase and distributed them. All the recipients ripped their envelopes open greedily as soon as Mr. Elmira handed them over. It was clear they expected them to contain money.

"Wow," David murmured. "It sure doesn't look like they're dying of grief."

"Yeah, they're only interested in the money," Lily said with a sigh.

"But I have a feeling Dr. Horton is about to play a little trick on them," Josh said with a smile.

"What do you mean?" David and Lily asked.

"Do you notice anything strange?"

 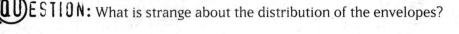 **QUESTION:** What is strange about the distribution of the envelopes?

CLUE THREE: Detached Pieces

Josh carefully counted the envelopes as the attorney handed them out. There were seven in all, but there were eight people at the table. Someone was missing an envelope!

The unlucky person turned out to be a distant cousin of Dr. Horton's, a man with sideburns who quickly realized he was the only one without an envelope. He got up, muttering under his breath, bowed stiffly to the rest of the group, and left, slamming the door behind him.

"What a bad sport!" Lily murmured.

But even the people who had received envelopes looked disappointed. All the envelopes contained were torn-up scraps of paper. Each scrap of paper had a totally incomprehensible message on it. The heirs threw their pieces of paper on the table.

"Aunt Amelia was crazy!" cried the woman in black. "She spent her whole life coming up with silly games like this. She loved this kind of thing!"

"If you wouldn't mind," Mr. Elmira interjected, "I think that the deceased wished for you to put those scraps of paper together to make one message."

Dr. Horton's relatives looked at the pieces of paper strewn across the table, confused.

"I get it," David whispered to his friends. "Do you want me to tell you what the message says?"

Lily and Josh nodded excitedly. Of course they wanted to know!

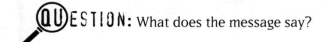 **QUESTION:** What does the message say?

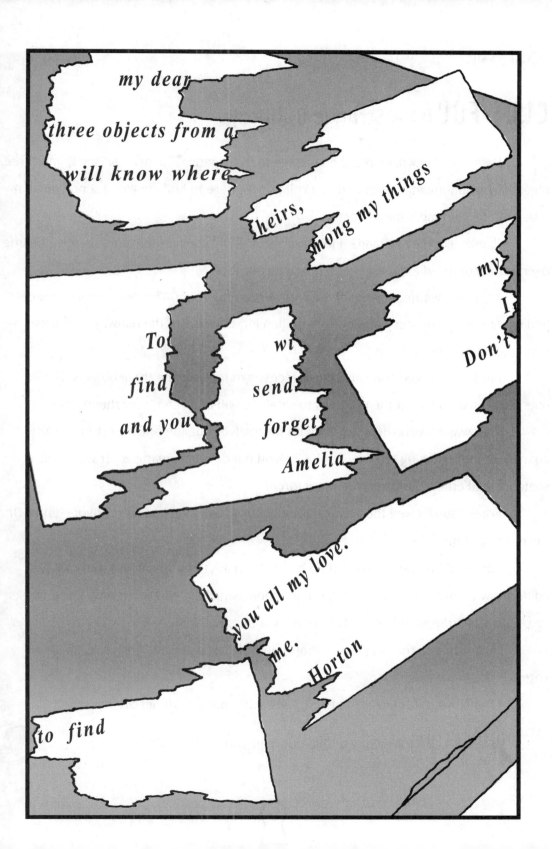

CLUE FOUR: A Strange Robbery

David quietly whispered the message to his friends: "'To my dear heirs, find three objects from among my things and you will know where to find my will. I send you all my love. Don't forget me. Amelia Horton.'"

"Looks like they've made a lot of progress," Lily commented sarcastically, looking over at the confused expressions on the relatives' faces.

Tony was waiting for the detectives outside the room. The detectives snuck out and explained the mystery to him. Tony pulled Mr. Elmira into the hallway to discuss what the detectives had said.

Mr. Elmira asked Tony and the detectives to look for the three objects in question—he didn't want the relatives to steal the will and keep it for themselves.

That was how the detectives found themselves outside of Dr. Horton's empty apartment the following afternoon. The lock on the door was mangled. It looked as if someone had entered the apartment by force!

Frank interviewed the next-door neighbor to ask if he had seen anyone enter Dr. Horton's apartment.

The neighbor explained that he hadn't seen anything suspicious, but that he *could* show them a photograph of her living room, which he had taken only a few weeks ago. That way they would know if anything was missing.

"According to the neighbor's photo, nothing has changed," Josh said upon entering the living room.

"That's what it seems like at first," Lily said. "But two things are missing."

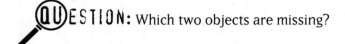 **QUESTION:** Which two objects are missing?

CLUE FIVE: The Phantom Painting

"Good job, Lily! You're right!" David cried. "The pipe that was hanging on the wall and the statuette by the window are both missing!"

"It looks like the statue is a Vapide," Josh added. "They're really expensive!"

After spending a few more minutes investigating without any leads, the detectives decided to leave the apartment. Suddenly, David noticed one more troubling detail. He pointed out a strange mark on the wallpaper.

"It looks like there used to be a painting hanging here."

Lily proposed that the detectives head over to the nearby Otto Matt Gallery to look for clues.

"You'd have to be pretty stupid to sell a painting right down the street from where you'd stolen it," Josh said.

"Maybe our thief was in a hurry?" Lily suggested.

The detectives arrived at the gallery a few minutes later. It was hard to spot any clues because the walls were entirely covered with paintings! On top of that, the detectives weren't even sure what they were looking for. The only clue they had was the mark the painting had left on the wall. After quickly inspecting the premises, David located the painting and rushed over to tell his friends.

"Look, guys! Dr. Horton's painting is here!"

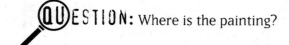 **QUESTION:** Where is the painting?

CLUE SIX: An Absentminded Painter

David pointed toward a painting in the corner, partly hidden behind an easel. It was sandwiched between a portrait of a woman wearing a hat and a landscape of a sunset over the countryside. The painting was a portrait of a man sitting in an armchair. To tell the truth, it was really nothing special.

The detectives questioned Otto Matt about the painting. He was very embarrassed to learn that he had a stolen painting in his gallery.

"I bought it five days ago, but I didn't know it was stolen, I assure you—I thought it was basically worthless!"

"So it's not even valuable?" Josh asked, stunned.

"The frame is worth a lot more than the portrait. I only bought it because it was offered to me for a great price. I didn't even think it was a good painting!"

"Well, it *is* a pretty terrible painting . . ." David commented.

"I don't think it's so bad!" Josh protested.

"Humph! It's the work of an amateur! It looks like he painted it with his toes!" the gallery owner responded.

"That's a bit of an exaggeration, Mr. Matt," Lily said. "But it's true that it isn't very well done."

"What are you talking about?" Josh asked, dumbstruck. "I would love to be able to paint like that!"

"Look closely," Lily told Josh. "The painter made a pretty serious error that he wouldn't have made if he had paid closer attention to his model."

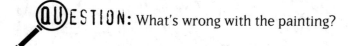 **QUESTION:** What's wrong with the painting?

CLUE SEVEN: The First Clue

Josh stared hard at the painting, but he still couldn't see what Lily was talking about. She pointed out that the stripes on the man's tie were all facing the same direction, even on the knot. But that was impossible—the stripes on the knot of a necktie always face the opposite direction from the stripes on the rest of the tie.

"My goodness! You have a sharp eye, my girl. Even I didn't notice that!" cried Otto Matt.

The three friends inspected the painting closely. Maybe the three objects that had been stolen from the apartment were the same three objects mentioned in Horton's will.

The portrait didn't seem to hold any secrets. David flipped the painting over to look at its back. A torn piece of paper was stuck between the frame and the canvas. David pulled the paper out and was quickly disappointed by what he saw. Again, Dr. Horton had divided her message into three pieces, each incomprehensible on its own.

Lily sighed. "Mr. Matt, do you remember the person who sold you this painting?"

"Ah, yes! That much I do remember. She was a blond woman, wearing a pair of cat's-eye glasses."

The detectives thanked the gallery owner and decided to find Tony and Frank and show them the precious scrap of paper. Josh proposed that they first grab a bite to eat at the café in the big department store across the street. The detectives were hungry—they hadn't eaten anything all day. But they got a lot more than a couple of sandwiches: As soon as they walked into the store, they saw a woman who matched Otto Matt's description perfectly!

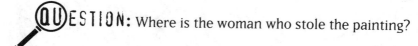 **QUESTION:** Where is the woman who stole the painting?

CLUE EIGHT: One Lost, One Found

"I'll bet that's the woman who stole the portrait!" Josh cried. "Quick, follow me!"

He led his friends toward the elevator where he had spotted the woman. The detectives hurried over, but the elevator doors closed just as they got there. They had no way of knowing which floor the woman was going to, so they decided to search every floor.

They began their search in the perfume department. There was no sign of the woman there, so the detectives decided to split up to search the rest of the store. But no matter how many times they walked around the store, there was still no sign of the woman. The store was about to close, so the detectives reluctantly decided to give up.

"Wait! There! It's her!" Josh cried.

Josh had caught a glimpse of the woman just as she was leaving the store, carrying a shopping bag. David had just enough time to read what it said on her bag: *K. Lotte's Colors.*

"The paint company! But why would she be buying paint? Do you think it has something to do with the portrait?" David wondered aloud.

"That's exactly what we have to find out," Lily replied. "But we can't let her escape again!"

The detectives followed the woman out of the store and into the street, but they quickly lost sight of her in the crowd. Josh was furious.

"Oh, no! We almost had her!"

"Calm down," David said. "I know where she is, but we have to hurry."

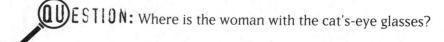 **QUESTION:** Where is the woman with the cat's-eye glasses?

CLUE NINE: Dock Dash

The woman with the glasses had just climbed into a taxi. David noticed the woman's shopping bag in the back window of the cab. The detectives jumped onto the next bus they saw, hoping that the Saturday night traffic wouldn't hold them up too much and they'd be able to follow the taxi. They also hoped that the taxi was heading in the same direction as their bus. Happily for them, they spotted the taxi in the sea of other cars on the road just as it was about to make a turn. Josh turned to David and Lily.

"She's going to the marina! We have to get off this bus!"

But they couldn't jump off the bus while it was still moving, so they had to wait until the next stop. They ran the few blocks from the bus stop back to the marina as quickly as they could. The detectives arrived just in time to see the woman exchange a few words with a strange man before following him into a warehouse.

The detectives were too afraid to risk being caught inside the spooky warehouse, so they hid behind a small sailboat docked nearby. But they couldn't see much from their hiding place.

"What are they plotting in there?" asked Josh, who was growing impatient.

"I think I know," Lily replied with a smile. "Do you?"

 **QUESTION:** 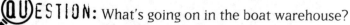 What's going on in the boat warehouse?

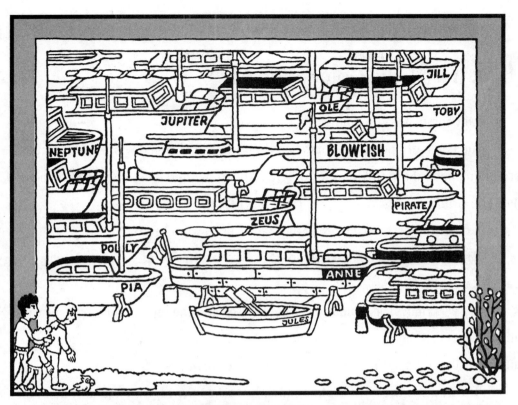

CLUE TEN: The Golden *Blowfish*

"Of course! They're painting!"

The name of one of the boats had mysteriously changed while the detectives were hiding behind the sailboat. *Blowfish* had been painted over, and now the boat was called the *Goldfish*!

"I don't understand why they did that," David wondered.

"The *Blowfish* must have been part of Dr. Horton's estate. I think they're going to steal it!" Lily said.

Lily was right. The woman with the glasses and the mysterious stranger were using the cover of night to put the *Goldfish* into the water. Then they climbed into a waiting car that quickly sped off in the direction of town.

"Did you see the license plate number?" asked David, who had only seen the first few characters.

"It's okay," Josh said. "All we need is the first few numbers. If we give them to Frank, he'll find out whose car it is."

The car was registered under the name of Mr. Jeremy Crabb, who lived at 82 Belleview Road.

The three friends met up with Frank and Tony in front of Crabb's apartment building early the next morning.

"There's no Jeremy Crabb here," David announced after looking at all of the mailboxes and doorbells.

"There is, too," Josh corrected him. "You just didn't look closely enough."

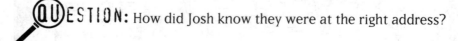 **QUESTION:** How did Josh know they were at the right address?

CLUE ELEVEN: A Wrong Turn

In the parking lot next to the building, Josh had noticed a parking spot designated for a car with the same license plate number they had spotted the night before.

The group circled the building, and Tony noticed a door marked CRABB. They knocked on the door several times.

"Police! Open up!"

A woman's voice sounded from inside the apartment. "Just a moment, please!" she called out sweetly.

They waited five whole minutes before the woman finally opened the door. The detectives weren't very surprised to find themselves face-to-face with the woman with the cat's-eye glasses. Tony asked her for ID, and she handed him her driver's license.

"Ms. Amy Geyser," Tony read aloud as he inspected her ID. "You were spotted last night at the marina repainting a boat that does not belong to you in order to steal it."

"Sir, I'm very sorry, but I think you're mistaken. Here. Look for yourself."

Amy Geyser leaned on her cane and carefully lifted up her left foot, which was in a cast up to her knee.

"I broke my ankle three days ago, and I can assure you that I haven't left the apartment since. I've been in too much pain."

"She's a bad actress!" David whispered in Tony's ear. "Her facts don't line up at all!"

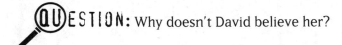 QUESTION: Why doesn't David believe her?

CLUE TWELVE: The Barbarian

Amy Geyser claimed she had broken her left ankle, but she was holding her cane in her right hand! If her left ankle was really injured, she would have been holding the cane in her left hand.

Tony decided to pretend he didn't notice anything suspicious.

"We must be mistaken, ma'am. Please excuse us."

Tony certainly wasn't fooled by her story, but he told the detectives that he thought it would be wiser to pretend he believed her story so she wouldn't become suspicious. It would be easier to follow her that way.

The detectives, Frank, and Tony pretended to leave and went back to their car to watch her from a distance. Forty-five minutes later, Amy snuck out of the apartment. She hailed a cab, and the detectives followed her in their car.

The taxi stopped in front of the Barbarian, a café in the neighborhood. Amy Geyser hurried inside.

"What could she be doing in there?" Frank asked.

"Patience, Frank," Tony said, following her inside. "We'll know soon enough."

But Tony had spoken too soon: The thief was nowhere to be seen!

"This woman is quite a chameleon!" Lily exclaimed.

"A chameleon with cat's-eye glasses . . . luckily for us!" joked Josh, who had just spotted her.

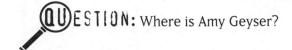 **QUESTION:** Where is Amy Geyser?

CLUE THIRTEEN: The Classifieds

Amy was in another room, behind a counter. Josh had spotted her reflection on the window. She was talking to a man.

A few minutes later, the man left the room holding one of the two little bags Amy had been carrying. He then walked up to the counter and ordered a coffee.

"Police," Tony said, walking up to the man and flashing his badge. Tony ordered the man to empty his bag.

Inside the bag was the little statuette that had disappeared from Horton's apartment!

"You must know that this object was stolen," Tony said.

The stranger remained silent, so Tony and Frank decided to take him to the police station for further questioning.

David, Josh, and Lily were put in charge of keeping an eye on Amy Geyser while Tony and Frank were gone. After a few minutes, Amy left the café. The detectives watched as Amy entered a phone booth and shut the door.

Josh quietly crept up to the phone booth to spy; Amy Geyser took out a newspaper and flipped through the pages. Then she dialed a number on the phone. The conversation didn't last long, and she hurriedly left the phone booth, leaving behind her newspaper. As soon as the coast was clear, the three detectives pounced on it.

"She dialed a nine and then a one. Those were the only things I could see," Josh reported.

"Don't worry about it, Josh! I think I have the right number!" Lily announced.

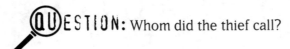 **QUESTION:** Whom did the thief call?

Nightly News

Friday

Exchange antique side table for antique armoire. Call 555-1342.

Seeking cell phone, $50 max. Call 555-3949 after 6 pm.

Louis XV bureau for sale, call: 555-1766.

We buy model trains and cars. Call 555-3343.

eeking 3rd Century Gallo-Roman coins. **Please call: 555-8765.**

Retired jeweler seeks vintage jewelry. Call 555-2124.

Check out our collection of gorgeous colonial stamps. 555-9798.

rgent! 30's bedroom set for sale. rice negotiable. Call 555-3409.

Needed: piano suitable for beginner. Call: 555-8009.

or sale: washing machine, some repairs necessary. 555-3501.

ust inherited valuables? Antiques xpert will evaluate and purchase valuable pieces! Call (191) 329-8181.

Discount furniture. Call: 555-1887. WHOLESALE!

Beautiful antique wooden toys for sale, Call 555-9908.

British Empire postcards for sale. Call 666-5757.

NEEDED: OTH CENTURY STUFFED ANIMALS. PLEASE CALL: 555-8212.

HUGE VIDEO GAME SALE!! TO SIGN UP, CALL: 555-1345.

For Sale: the complete set of "The Happy Knitter" magazines. Call: 555-4321.

The Kiddie Soccer League seeks goalie for school-wide championship. Call Matt LeDribble at 555-9783.

I just moved, and have boxes to spare. Call John Vanton at 555-6432.

I'M LEAVING FOR GREENLAND, and need to sell my fridge, complete with freezer and ice-maker. Call 555-9832.

Collector offering great prices on quality antiques. Call: 555-1488.

Billiard table for sale. Good condition, one ball missing. 555-9909.

Your friendly local firemen seek tango band for annual Fireman's Ball. See Fire Chief at 18 Hissel Street.

SEEKING: canopy bed for two, pastels preferred. Call Rose Tender at 555-6331.

SILVER JEWELRY FOR SALE. Contact Alfredo Romano at 555-1613.

FOR SALE: wooden horse figurines. Call Tom at 555-8891.

Crafting Competition. Prizes include hams, decorative baskets, etc. Speak to Mrs. Cook at 555-4756.

NEEDED: Male pony. Call 555-1883.

Urgent! Space heater needed. Call: 555-4423, ask for Geoffrey.

FOR SALE: AUTHENTIC COO-COO CLOCK FROM SWITZERLAND. CALL 555-9989.

Antiques in perfect condition call 555-6012.

Seeking professional lumberjack Contact G. Depak at 555-6180.

FOR SALE: wedding dress, size 12. Brand new. 555-0098.

Help me find my garden gnomes. They disappeared from my yard last Wednesday. Snow White and are devastated. 555-9388.

FOUND: 5 GARDEN GNOMES. CALL 555-1518.

WE'RE CLOSING, NEED TO SELL A BIG AQUARIUM FULL OF EXOTIC FISH. COME BY THE GOLDEN FISH RESTAURAN

Amateur theater company seeks volunteer costume designer. 555

SPORTS SUPPLY STORE OPENING! GRAND OPENING SALES UNTIL THE END OF JUNE!! CALL 555-4142.

Discover the mysteries of magic. Call the Illusionist Club at 555-7777.

The Film Society needs a castle, preferably with drawbridge, turrets, and a carriage. 555-0010.

Family station wagon for sale Easy payments. 555-1973.

Elementary School seeks children's book author to teach writing seminar. Call Principal Smith at 555-8213.

CLUE FOURTEEN: Fight!

The announcement read: *Just inherited valuables? Antiques expert will evaluate and purchase valuable pieces! Call (191) 329-8181.* That must have been the number Amy dialed!

Lily quickly called the number. But all she heard on the other end was a message: "Francis Amber Stadium. Today at 3 P.M., the Clash of the Titans: Didi Lapolle against Sammy Carhart."

"That's the boxing arena," Lily explained as she hung up. "What time is it?"

"Two-forty," David replied, looking at his watch.

"Perfect! That leaves us just enough time to get there."

The three detectives arrived at the stadium just in time for the match. When Josh, David, and Lily got to the ticket window, they were surprised to see that Amy Geyser was standing right in front of them, buying her ticket for the fight.

"Somehow I don't think she's here for fun . . ." David commented as he bought their tickets.

The fight had just begun, and the crowd was cheering the boxers on. It was dark inside the arena, so the detectives lost sight of Amy Geyser again.

The detectives searched the stands for any sign of her. Eventually, they spotted her in the crowd. At that exact moment, she was handing the second little bag over to someone in exchange for a large wad of bills.

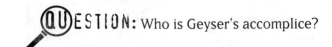 **QUESTION:** Who is Geyser's accomplice?

CLUE FIFTEEN: Pipe Dream

Amy Geyser was sitting just below the emergency exit sign and had just made a deal with the mustached man sitting in front of her.

"That's definitely Dr. Horton's pipe," David murmured.

After Amy finished handing over the pipe, she quickly left her seat and hurried out of the arena. The man with the mustache, however, seemed interested in the fight. He waited until Carhart had won before standing and heading up the stairs.

The detectives followed him and eventually found themselves in front of a door marked FRANCIS AMBER, DIRECTOR. They hesitated, unsure whether to knock on the door or not. But they didn't have to make a decision. The man with the mustache noticed them first.

"Come in! You're the famous detectives! To what do I owe the honor of your visit?"

The detectives were shocked at how friendly the man was. He seemed trustworthy and honest, so they decided to tell him the story about Amelia Horton's will and the three thefts.

"I knew the price I paid for that pipe seemed too good to be true!" Francis Amber said. "I'm sorry, kids, I thought I was just getting a good deal. I had no idea it was stolen!" Francis Amber had a very large pipe collection in his office. The detectives had trouble recognizing Horton's pipe, which they had only seen for a moment, among all the others. Josh finally found it.

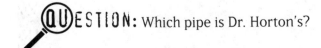 **QUESTION:** Which pipe is Dr. Horton's?

CLUE SIXTEEN: Masks Off!

Francis Amber took the pipe down. It was hanging to the left of the clock.

He gave the pipe back to the detectives, who then hurried out of the arena and back to the police station to hand the pipe over to Tony as evidence.

Then they decided it was time to deal with Amy Geyser, so Tony, Frank, and the three detectives went back to her apartment.

While Tony knocked on her door, Lily peeked at Amy Geyser's garbage. *You could learn a lot about a person by looking through their trash*, Lily thought. She lifted the lid of the garbage can and was surprised at what she saw: a pair of cat's-eye glasses and a blond wig!

The door to the apartment finally opened, and standing there was Rita Hartford! It was the same woman in black who had introduced herself as Amelia Horton's niece during the reading of the will. The detectives couldn't believe it, but Amy Geyser and Rita Hartford were the same person! Tony immediately arrested the woman for falsifying documents—her ID said she was Amy Geyser, after all—as well as for the theft of the brooch, the painting, the statuette, the pipe, and the boat, which were all a part of her aunt's inheritance. Rita Hartford grudgingly handed over the two remaining pieces of the message, which she had found inside the pipe and the statuette.

The detectives finally had all the pieces of the puzzle. All they had to do was put them together and they would have Dr. Horton's will.

"I've got it!" David announced after putting the pieces of paper in order.

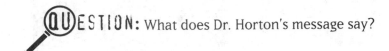 **QUESTION:** What does Dr. Horton's message say?

Look ... in the attic.
the ... loot ... is not
far ... from ... the watering can

CLUE ONE: A Dog's Life

The message read: *Look in the attic. The loot is not far from the watering can.*

The detectives hurried to Dr. Horton's, where David easily spotted the treasure among all the antiques in Horton's attic. Sitting on a shelf next to a watering can was an old jewelry box that contained several pieces of gold, as well as Dr. Horton's will.

"Wow, you did it! Good job!" exclaimed the man working at the dog shelter after the friends told him the whole story two days later.

The detectives had recently learned that, to the horror of her relatives, Dr. Horton had left her entire fortune to the local dog shelter. Amelia Horton had played a trick on her relatives, but it turned out that they deserved it.

Rita Hartford was outraged when she heard the news.

"Oh, if only I'd found that scrap of paper hidden in the painting! I wouldn't be here today if I had!"

"Here" was the jail at the police station, where she was locked up, awaiting her trial.

The detectives were celebrating their victory with the amused guard at the dog shelter when a man appeared, looking for his dog. The man said his name was Ronald Newsom.

"He has three black spots on his back," Newsom told the detectives.

"Lucky for us he doesn't have four," Lily joked as she pointed to the missing dog, "or else it would have been a lot harder to find him."

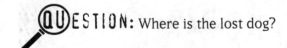 **QUESTION:** Where is the lost dog?

CLUE TWO: Suspicious . . .

The dog was near the fence, next to a tree. He looked like he was waiting for someone to come get him.

The shelter employee retrieved the missing dog. He spoke briefly with the man before handing the dog over.

"Mr. Newsom, can you tell me your address?"

"Sure," the man said cautiously. "13 Park Street."

The guard nodded and handed over the dog. "Pay better attention next time," he recommended.

"Yeah, yeah," Newsom muttered. "Come on, Sparky." He left quickly.

"I don't like him very much," Lily told the guard after Newsom had left.

The detectives said good-bye to the guard and started back to the Sugar Shack.

"Do you think he was actually the owner of that dog?" Lily asked.

"The dog wouldn't have let him take him if he weren't."

"I don't know," David said. "The dog seemed a little lost when Newsom took him away. Lily might be right. What do you think, Robinson?"

But Robinson was upset and distracted. The group had just paused in front of a pet shop, and Robinson hated seeing birds in cages. He flapped his wings and flew off toward the trees. Josh turned to see where Robinson went, but became distracted by signs posted on the tree trunks.

"Hey! You were right! That wasn't his dog!"

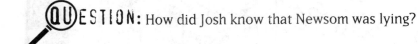 **QUESTION:** How did Josh know that Newsom was lying?

CLUE THREE: Three Scoops

Josh had spotted an announcement on a tree trunk with a photo of the dog in question. It read: *Who Stole Puffin? Help me find him. Reward.* The missing dog's name was Puffin, but Mr. Newsom had called him Sparky.

"That's horrible!" Lily cried. "To think that we saw this crime happening and didn't realize it!"

"I hope he doesn't hurt him," Josh said. "If he does, he'll have to answer to me!" Josh loved animals.

"Do you remember the address that Newsom gave the guard?" David asked.

"Park Street, I think," Lily guessed.

"That's it! 13 Park Street! Do you know where that is?" Josh asked.

"Not exactly," David answered. "But I have an idea."

David decided that the detectives needed a pick-me-up before pursuing the thief. They ducked into a nearby ice-cream parlor to grab a treat. They sat outside on the terrace, which looked out over the whole neighborhood. David asked the man behind the counter for a map of the city, which he promptly handed over to Josh. While Josh studied the map, David looked out at the view of the town. He eventually found Park Street before Josh did.

"Forget it, Josh, I found it. Unfortunately, it won't do us very much good to go there. Ronald Newsom is definitely crafty . . ."

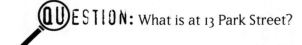 **QUESTION:** What is at 13 Park Street?

CLUE FOUR: Robinson's Discovery

Number 13 Park Street was actually a flower shop! Even though it was a fake address, they decided to talk to the florist anyway.

"Excuse me, sir. Do you know a man named Ronald Newsom?" the detectives asked the man in the flower shop a few minutes later.

"No, I'm sorry, kids. That name doesn't sound familiar at all, and I've been in this spot for two years now."

Disappointed, the three detectives left the florist.

"It breaks my heart to think that there's nothing we can do for that poor little dog!" Josh said on the way back to the Sugar Shack.

"Don't worry, Josh," Lily said. "I'm sure if we think hard enough, we can figure out where he is."

But back at the Sugar Shack, they still couldn't think of any ideas. Just when they were about to give up, Robinson flew through the window holding a strange-looking cookie in his beak.

"That's not a cookie—it's a dog biscuit! Robinson, where did you find that?" David asked his loyal cockatoo.

Robinson squawked and made circles in the air to signal that the detectives should follow him. Five minutes later, the detectives were staring into an abandoned lot.

"It's like a jungle in there! How are we supposed to see what you're trying to show us?"

Robinson continued to fly around; he knew that more dog biscuits were in there.

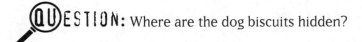 **QUESTION:** Where are the dog biscuits hidden?

CLUE FIVE: A Trap

In the middle of the abandoned lot was a tree with a broken trunk. Someone had stashed dog biscuits inside the trunk. They must have been left there for the neighborhood's homeless dogs.

"Do you think someone is taking care of all the stray dogs?" Josh asked.

"I doubt it," David answered. "I think someone is trying to attract dogs to this area on purpose."

"David's right," said Lily. "Someone who was actually concerned about the dogs would have left them something more nutritious to eat, like meat or kibble."

When they approached the tree trunk, the detectives noticed that a trap had been rigged above the food. Once a dog climbed inside the trunk to eat the biscuits, a cage would fall down on it.

"What do you think happens to the dogs once they're captured?" Josh asked grimly.

"I'm afraid to find out," David said. "But maybe if we hide in the bushes, we'll catch the crook in the act." Josh and Robinson agreed, but Lily was wary.

"It's not a bad idea," she told David, "but it'll take a while, and there's no point in trying to do it today."

"Why not?"

"Because whoever is catching these dogs isn't going to be so easy to catch. In fact, he's watching us right now."

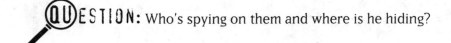 **QUESTION:** Who's spying on them and where is he hiding?

CLUE SIX: Lucky Break

Lily could see a pair of shoes sticking out of the doorway of number 37.

"I have a feeling we've found Ronald Newsom. He was wearing those exact same shoes," David whispered.

"It all makes sense now," Josh murmured.

The detectives quietly snuck up to the building where they had spotted the man. By the time they got there, the man was already gone.

"This is all that's left of him," Lily noted as she picked two matches up off the ground. One match was half-burned, but the other one looked brand-new.

"Luckily, he broke one of the matches without managing to light it," said David. "With any luck, we'll be able to find out where it came from."

"Good point," said Josh. "There can't be too many places that give out all-white matches."

The detectives were optimistic because Francis Amber, the pipe enthusiast, had given them a large collection of matchbooks on the day they met him at the boxing arena. The designs were beautiful, and the matchbooks were collectible. Maybe one of them had matches that looked like the one they just found!

They hurried back to the Sugar Shack and spread the boxes of matches out on the table to examine them. David finally found the correct matchbook.

 **QUESTION:** Where did the matches they found come from?

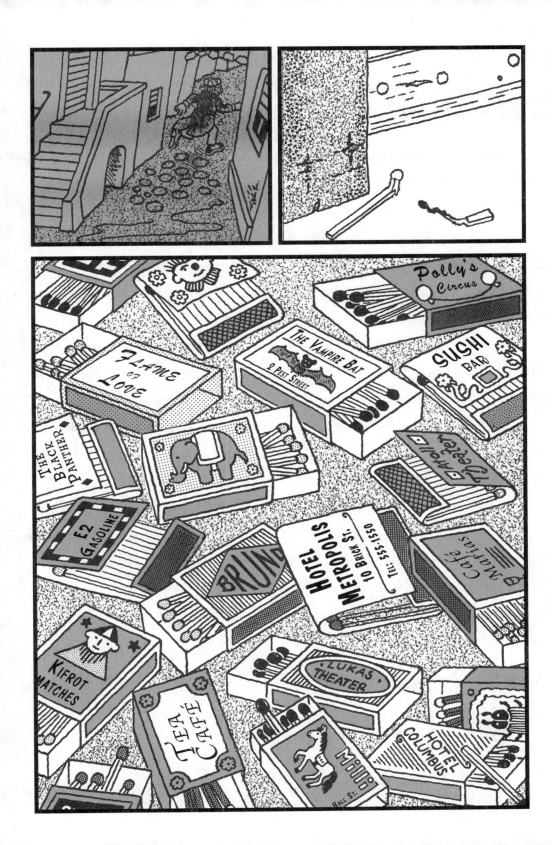

CLUE SEVEN: The Black Panther

The matches came from a café called The Black Panther. The address was printed on the back of the matchbook.

It was too late to visit the café that night, so the detectives decided to postpone their trip until the following evening. The café was sure to be packed, and they could slip in without being seen. They hoped to obtain information about Ronald Newsom. If he went to The Black Panther a lot, they could probably learn something about him from one of the other customers.

The next night, on their way to the café, the three detectives tried to come up with a believable story to explain why they had so many questions about Newsom. They didn't want the other customers at The Black Panther to become suspicious of them!

"If we're lucky, we won't need a story," Josh said. "Maybe Newsom will be there himself!"

"Yeah, right, Josh. That plan seems a little *too* easy," Lily said, teasing.

"You never know, Lily," David said. "We've had a lot of luck so far in this case."

Once they arrived at the café, Josh, David, and Lily peeked through the window of the café to see if Newsom was inside. Josh sighed.

"Lily was right after all. He's not here."

"He is, too! I *was* wrong! Newsom is here; I see him. We don't even need to go inside to keep an eye on him."

 **QUESTION:** Where is Ronald Newsom?

CLUE EIGHT: Rendezvous

Ronald Newsom was sitting in front of the café, perched on a stool. He was wearing the same shoes and cap that he had on the day the detectives met him at the animal shelter.

Lily and David stood at the curb and pretended they were waiting for the bus, while Josh walked a safe distance away from the café and took out his binoculars to spy on Newsom. He watched the waiter hand Newsom a theater ticket. He could just make out what was written on the ticket: *May 13, at 3 P.M.* Josh rushed over to David and Lily and told them the news.

"That's great, but we have no idea which show it is," David said.

"Or where it is," Lily added.

"Let's go back to the Sugar Shack," David proposed. "We'll have better luck researching the show there."

"We have to work fast—the thirteenth is tomorrow!" Josh cried.

On the way back to their headquarters, the detectives stopped at a newsstand and bought a copy of the *Nightly News*. Their plan was to look through the Leisure and Outings section for any mention of an event on the thirteenth. As soon as they got back to the Sugar Shack, they began scouring the paper for information.

"There it is! I found it!" cried Josh; he had been concentrating on the task the entire time.

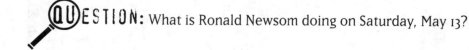 **QUESTION:** What is Ronald Newsom doing on Saturday, May 13?

Regional Miniature Golf Championship. The sporting complex: May 14 at 1 P.M. Greens fee: $5

The Marvelous Mountains Club will climb Berger's Hill. May 13 at 7 A.M. Meet at Star Square. We'll return at 3 P.M. Sandwiches provided. $15 all included.

Ripton Fairgrounds Festival from May 12-15. Many attractions for young and old.

Argenton Village welcomes The Amazing Zilesco! Meet the famous magician and see him perform feats of wonder and daring. The Village Green. May 13, 7 P.M. In case of rain, meet at the Textile Museum.

Dutch folk dancing. Come learn traditional steps. Followed by a tasting of cheeses from Holland. May 13, from 6 P.M. in the square in front of the town hall.

Hot air balloon ride. The Wright Stuff Flying Field. May 13 at 9 A.M. (weather permitting). Adults: $35. Family rate: $50. Admire your town from the air!

Mushroom Festival. Rambeau Forest. Organized by the Mycological Association Meeting point: Diana Square, May 14 at 8 A.M.

Dinner Theater aboard the *Siren* **with the Ulysses Band.** Greek music and gorgeous scenery guaranteed. Departing from Pier Three. May 13 at 8 P.M. sharp. Return at 11 P.M.

Painting exhibition, open call for artists and art lovers. Show your work and admire the work of others. May 13 at 2 P.M. at the Public Gardens. In case of rain, meet at the town hall. Prizes awarded from 2-3 P.M.

Spring sale at the Grand Salon May 13 from 7 A.M. to 5 P.M. Alice Martin Way location.

Bowling Tournament. May 14 from 10 A.M. to 6 P.M. Awards presentation from 6-6:30. Academy Lanes, Smithson Field Road.

Lecture: "Howling with the Wind" The celebrated adventurer Martina Oleska explains her frightening adventures in her solo sailing trip around the world. Nautical Club. May 14, 3 P.M.

An Open Book. Join us for a lecture at the Public Garden by Cheryl Lawrence, who will speak on her recent novel, *The Dandelion Gang.* May 13 at 4 P.M.

Cooking Class. Learn to prepare a delicious lingonberry tart with Swedish Chef Lars Hiaasen. Materials fee: $10. May 14 at 3 P.M. at the Star.

Focus on Safety. The Department of Transportation sponsors this refresher on the rules of the road for cyclists. Ages 8 and up welcome. Saturday May 13 from 10-12. At Greyson Elementary School parking lot. Bring your bikes.

Dog Show. For all ages. The Furry Friends Club hosts. May 13 at 3 P.M. at the Blue Arena. Many prizes in all categories. Public admission: $12. Free for competitors.

Terrace of Miley Mansion. *The Orphan and the Thief* with Laura Feder and Brice Classon. From May 13-16 at 8 P.M. Tickets at the door or call 555-1303.

Open Air Theater. Screening film classic *The Red Horse of the Samurai* At The Clamshell in Baker's Park. May 16 at 9 P.M.

"China Faces Its Future" Photo exhibition followed by panel discussion. Moderator Arnold Durand. Cultural Center. May 13. 6 P.M. Free to the public.

Huge sale on oriental carpets. Exceptional quality, low prices. May 13 from 9-3 P.M. Hotel Four Winds. Free entry. All-you-can-eat buffet: $15.

Scavenger Hunt. City-wide search for treasures, organized by the planning board. May 14 at 3 P.M. All are welcome. Meet at the starting point: Lavelle Road.

CLUE NINE: Puppy Parade

The next afternoon, the detectives walked over to the Dog Show. When they arrived, the exposition was already packed with people—and dogs! The event was like an annual playdate for all the dogs in town. The dogs that had been to the event before ran around happily, tails wagging, looking for their doggie friends.

The three detectives walked toward the podium, where the participants in the Puppy Parade were lining up.

They watched as the first contestants walked around the stage. Lily tried not to nod off—she thought the Dog Show was pretty boring. All the puppies' owners seemed tense—they each really wanted to win the competition—but all the dogs looked like they were having a lot of fun.

At the exact moment the commentator was announcing a happy yellow Labrador named Kane, a scream rang out. A hush fell over the crowd of people.

Josh, David, and Lily watched as a weeping woman ran from the room holding a leash that had been cut. Someone had stolen her dog in the middle of the show!

"It looks like Ronald Newsom didn't waste any time," David remarked.

"Let's go ask the woman for a description of her dog," Josh suggested. "I'm sure we can find him."

"There's no need," Lily said. "I saw the woman and her dog together earlier, and I remember what he looks like."

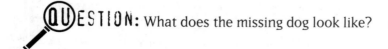 **QUESTION:** What does the missing dog look like?

CLUE TEN: Help!

The missing dog was white with black spots, just like little Puffin. Lily had noticed him earlier because he had a big red bow around his neck, which made him look pretty ridiculous.

The detectives set off to look for Ronald Newsom, even though they didn't think they'd be able to find him. It was crowded, and the exposition hall was gigantic.

"That guy's really starting to bug me. This is the second time he's slipped away with a poor innocent dog," Josh said.

"Don't worry, Josh. We'll do everything we can to make sure it doesn't happen again," Lily promised him.

"But first we have to find him," said David. "Where should we start?"

"The newspaper," Josh proposed. He had just picked one up from off the ground; it was crumpled up between a few empty soda cans and discarded candy bar wrappers. "Look, here's an article that might help." The first page was entirely dedicated to the dog thefts.

"'Another dog theft,'" Lily read. "Look! This dog was taken from the front of a supermarket!"

"You can even see the cut leash in the photo! Newsom is a pretty confident thief," David replied.

"He deserves a kick in the—" Josh was getting angry.

"Josh, be patient. He'll get what's coming to him."

"Wait, look at this!" David cried. "Newsom left more than the cut leash behind!"

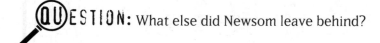 **QUESTION:** What else did Newsom leave behind?

THE MESSENGER

CLUE ELEVEN: Establishing a Pattern

"Good catch!" Lily said. "I never would have noticed that Newsom left the dog's collar under that dumpster."

The three detectives made their way over to the empty lot. The collar was still sitting exactly where it was in the photo. The name tag on the collar had the dog's name and address engraved on it, so Josh, David, and Lily hurried off to return the collar to its owner.

The dog's owner became hopeful that her dog would be found once the detectives told her they were on the case. She happily gave them a photo of her dog.

"No way!" Lily cried after looking at the photo. "It's the same kind of dog: white with black spots."

"This case is getting way out of hand. We—" Josh stopped and put his hand to his ear.

"What is it, Josh? Did you hear something?" David asked.

"Yes, I thought I heard someone screaming for help."

The detectives took off in the direction of the screams.

"Help! Thief! Someone took my little dog!"

Even though he already knew what the answer would be, David asked the tearful woman what her dog looked like.

"White, not very big, with black spots."

"This isn't a coincidence. I have a really bad feeling these kidnappings might have something to do with experiments in a lab . . ." But Lily never finished her sentence.

"Quick! Over there! I see the thief *and* the dog!"

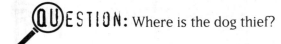 **QUESTION:** Where is the dog thief?

CLUE TWELVE: An Impasse

A man turned the corner near a pickup truck carrying a dog in his arms. Lily was sure that the man was Ronald Newsom. The three friends ran after him, but the street was crowded. The detectives couldn't catch up with the man and lost his trail.

A few minutes later, the detectives stopped in front of an empty alley and scratched their heads in confusion.

"He couldn't have just disappeared into thin air!" David cried.

"No, he can't be far from here. Maybe he went somewhere to hide," Lily guessed.

"What should we do now?" David asked.

"We stay here and wait," Josh said. "He has to come out sometime."

The detectives waited at the entrance to the alley. Josh checked his watch impatiently. Five minutes went by, then ten minutes, twenty minutes, and half an hour! After exactly thirty-two minutes, Ronald Newsom finally resurfaced.

"Oh, there he is! I don't believe it!" David said.

"Yeah, but where's the dog?" Josh wondered.

"I don't know. What could he have done with it in such a short amount of time? Where could he have left the poor dog?" Lily asked.

"Unfortunately, I can't tell you what he did with the dog, Lily, but I do know where Newsom went," Josh replied.

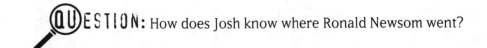 **QUESTION:** How does Josh know where Ronald Newsom went?

CLUE THIRTEEN: Newsom's New 'Do

"He just came out of that hair salon. Look, he's shaved his head!"

Josh was right. In the thirty-two minutes he was gone, Ronald Newsom had gotten himself a buzz cut so that when he came back out, the detectives wouldn't recognize him. Newsom sat down at an outdoor café, thinking the detectives would have no idea who he was. But he didn't realize that he was still wearing the same glasses and shoes from before, and his cap was sitting on the table.

Newsom hadn't even finished his root beer float when Frank and Tony arrived on the scene to arrest the thief. Lily had called her uncles, and they hurried over as soon as they could. After Tony and Frank apprehended Newsom, he pretended to be innocent, pleading that he was the victim of circumstances.

"We really need some evidence," Lily said to Josh and David.

"Maybe the hairstylist will know something," Josh suggested.

The detectives decided to check it out. "Hello, ma'am. How much for a haircut?" David said politely as the group walked into the hair salon, Curly Q's.

"Well, that depends," the stylist replied in an unfriendly tone. "With or without styling?"

"Uh . . . without, I guess."

"Do you also do dog grooming?" Josh asked awkwardly.

The stylist looked at him stonily. "No. Animals are strictly forbidden in the salon. And that goes for your bird—he needs to wait outside."

"She's charming," David muttered under his breath. "And what a liar!"

 **QUESTION:** How does David know the stylist is lying?

CLUE FOURTEEN: Saved!

The dog bone on the floor by the back door made David doubt the stylist. Unless the woman ate dog bones herself, it was a pretty clear indication that she'd had a canine visitor recently. They had to figure out what was behind that door before the stylist became suspicious.

David sat down in the stylist's chair for a haircut. Before she began, he asked if he could look at the salon's magazines to decide what kind of cut he wanted. Lily stayed with David to offer her advice, while Josh announced that he was going outside to keep Robinson company. But once the stylist started cutting David's hair, Josh snuck back into the salon toward the boarded-up back door. The door opened up into a dark room. Josh could hear desperate whimpers and low barks. The dogs!

"Shhh!" Josh told them. "If you aren't quiet, they'll find me! But don't worry, I'm going to get you out of here."

Josh's soothing and friendly voice had an amazing effect on the dogs. They immediately calmed down. After turning on the light, Josh counted the dogs and realized that all of the dogs that had been kidnapped recently were there! Josh saw dozens of bottles of pills and syringes on a shelf and realized that Lily was right—these dogs *were* a part of some cruel science experiment! Josh panicked when he noticed that one of the cages was empty. Had something happened to one of the dogs?

Whew! Josh found the dog only a moment later. He must have gotten scared when Josh entered the room and hid.

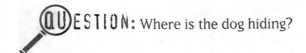 **QUESTION:** Where is the dog hiding?

CLUE ONE: A Noise in the Night

The dog was hiding behind a curtain, but after Josh whistled softly, the dog came out of his hiding place.

Josh found a secret exit and escaped. Once he was outside, he dialed Tony and Frank's number. They had just finished dropping Newsom off at the police station.

The stylist was putting the finishing touches on David's cut when Frank and Tony burst into the salon and arrested her. Animal Control followed right behind to rescue the dogs and return them to their families.

"You came just in time," David joked a while later as Tony drove the detectives home. "Five minutes more and I wouldn't have had any hair left!"

Everyone burst out laughing, except for Josh. He was listening intently and staring out the window.

"Did you guys hear that? I thought I heard a big splash! Maybe something happened at the bridge over there!"

Tony immediately pulled the car over and everyone jumped out. They took off toward the bridge but couldn't see anything splashing in the water. The detectives decided to get a closer look. They walked down by the water, but the only suspicious thing they saw was fresh tracks in the mud that looked like they were made by a horse-drawn carriage. Josh bent down to examine the tracks.

"So that's what it was! Maybe it fell from the carriage . . . Or rather, maybe someone threw it out . . ."

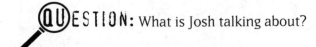 **QUESTION:** What is Josh talking about?

CLUE TWO: At the Fair

Josh had spotted a barrel floating in the reeds by the edge of the river. The detectives used a long stick to guide the barrel out of the water. Tony suggested that they send the barrel off to the lab for examination in case something dangerous was inside.

The next day, Josh, David, and Lily biked over to the police station for the lab results. Tony's suspicions were correct: The barrel contained a lethal poison!

"If we had only arrived a few minutes earlier, we could have caught the polluter red-handed," Lily said with a sigh.

"And now we have no way of ever figuring out who it was," Josh added dejectedly.

"Unless . . . Do you remember the tracks we saw on the riverbank? The hoofprints indicated that the horse pulling the carriage was missing half of the horseshoe on his left hind foot," David said.

"You call that a clue?" Josh asked.

"Don't give up so easily," David replied.

The three kids had a presentation due the following week, so they put the case aside and went back to the Sugar Shack to work. Lily came up with the great idea to do the project on the agricultural fair that was coming to town on Sunday.

The detectives went to the fair on Sunday to do research on chicken and pigs. The detectives were enjoying samples of local cheeses when Lily noticed something that almost made her choke on her sharp cheddar.

"Guys, look! I just saw the horse! We're back on the case!"

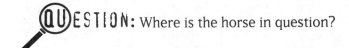 **QUESTION:** Where is the horse in question?

CLUE THREE: Umbrella Uncovered

Lily had seen a horse with only half a horseshoe trot past the stand marked PAUL & PAT. There was a procession of horses walking by, so the detectives lost sight of the horse with the missing horseshoe.

David was so determined to follow the horse that he was ready to jump on any nearby animal and chase it down, but he wasn't sure which way the horse and the carriage he was pulling had gone.

"What rotten luck! Did either of you see the driver's face?" he asked his friends.

"No, he was wearing a hood that covered his face," Lily replied. "Did you notice anything, Josh?"

"There was an umbrella in the carriage. It was yellow with purple polka dots. Though I don't think that will do us much good now."

Disappointed, the three detectives went back to tasting all the delicious foods that were on sale at the fair, hoping sweets would lift their spirits. But not even the honey-almond cake did the trick.

The detectives gave their presentation on the agricultural fair the following Wednesday, and it was a success. After school that day, Lily suggested that they visit the library to see if the new Agatha Kikri novel was out yet. David wasn't a big fan of the adventures of Hercules Navaro, but it was raining outside, and it was nice and dry in the library. Josh had a different idea: He wanted to dive back into the case.

"Put your books down, my friends, we have a mystery to solve! I think it's time to go out for a walk!"

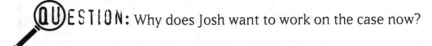 **QUESTION:** Why does Josh want to work on the case now?

CLUE FOUR: Pressure Cooker

"Yellow umbrellas with purple polka dots aren't very common," Josh told his friends. "And I just saw one leaving the bookstore and heading in that direction, toward the root beer factory. Let's go!"

The detectives dropped their books and ran over to the factory, but it was deserted once they got there.

The main room inside the factory was gigantic. It was filled with large vats of liquid and several loud machines. The factory was also filled with noise: the hum of motors, the whoosh of pumps, and the clanking of bottles on the conveyor belt.

The three detectives searched around the room while Robinson, frightened by the noise, perched on the corner of a desk that had a lot of buttons and switches on it.

"Don't touch any of them!" Lily warned him.

"It's cool that everything's done by robots, but it's weird that no one's here to oversee the machines," David remarked.

"You're right—it's weird *and* dangerous," Josh added.

The three friends called out, hoping that someone would answer. But no one responded.

"Maybe we should look for video cameras?" David asked.

"That won't be necessary, David. Someone is here, but we just haven't seen him yet," Lily said.

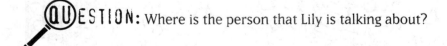 **QUESTION:** Where is the person that Lily is talking about?

CLUE FIVE: A Stagnant Search

Lily had spotted a hand removing one of the bottles from the conveyor belt. The detectives quietly crept up to the conveyor belt, where they came upon Peter Kruger, the owner of the root beer factory.

"You kids scared me!" he said, one hand gripping his chest. He motioned for them to follow him into a smaller room. "It's a lot quieter in here," he said once they were all inside. "So, what brings you kids to my factory?"

The detectives introduced themselves and explained why they were there.

"Really?" Peter Kruger asked, surprised. "Because someone stole a barrel from me about a month ago!"

"What a coincidence," Josh said. "Maybe it's the same barrel we found."

Kruger happily showed the detectives one of his barrels. It looked exactly like the one they had found in the river.

Unfortunately, this wasn't very much of a clue. It seemed unlikely that Mr. Kruger would use his own barrels to store toxic waste—it'd be too easy to catch him.

"Another dead end." Lily sighed.

The three friends thanked Peter Kruger and left the factory. On the way out, David found an odd-looking leaf on the ground and decided to take it home to add to his leaf collection.

Back at the Sugar Shack, David took out a large reference book to look up the name of the tree that the leaf had come from.

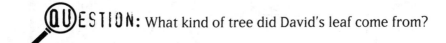

QUESTION: What kind of tree did David's leaf come from?

CLUE SIX: Rider's Repairs

"It's from a lemon tree!" David cried.

"That's strange," said Josh. "Lemon trees are rare around here because they can only grow indoors. I don't understand how this leaf could have gotten into the courtyard."

"It looks a little beat up," Lily remarked. "Maybe it got stuck on someone's shoe?"

"Or umbrella," David suggested.

"I think we've collected a lot of useless evidence: a broken horseshoe, a polka-dotted umbrella, a lemon tree leaf. It's not looking good, guys," Josh said.

"What do you say we take a break from the case for a while? Do you guys want to come with me while I pick up my bike?" Lily asked. "It's getting fixed right around the corner, at Don Rider's. It should be ready by now."

The boys agreed to go with Lily to pick up her bike. "Mmm, that smells good!" Josh said once they made it to the bike shop. "Something smells like lemon."

"That makes sense," said David. "Look up!"

There was a beautiful lemon tree growing in one corner of the courtyard.

"Another coincidence! And maybe another clue!" exclaimed Josh. "This is incredible!"

"Maybe not," said Lily. "But in any case, I wish I had never left my bike here. Some repairman! He doesn't know anything about bikes—look at what he did to my headlight!"

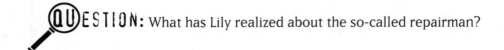

QUESTION: What has Lily realized about the so-called repairman?

CLUE SEVEN: A Strange Collection

"Did you see what he did to my headlight?" Lily asked, annoyed.

"Not really," Josh admitted.

"Look where he put it! Does that look normal to you?"

"You're right, Lily. That is weird," said David. "He put your headlight on the frame of the bike, not on the handlebars!"

"Yeah, that's practical! Now whenever I ride my bike at night, I'll be able to see the side of the road and not what's in front of me."

The fake repairman didn't seem to have much of a sense of humor.

"You got a problem?" he asked rudely.

Lily was about to complain about her bike, but David cut her off with a discreet nudge.

"Uh . . . no, it's . . . um . . . I'm here for my bike," she stammered.

"Well, what are you waiting for? Take it and get out of here!"

"Yes, sir . . ." Lily went to pick up her bike. Satisfied, Rider turned around and began to walk away. The boys took advantage of the time his back was turned to snoop around the courtyard a bit. The courtyard was filled with garbage and abandoned bicycle parts.

"I think we'd better get out of here," Lily advised after a few minutes had passed.

"You're right, Lily. But it doesn't surprise me that Don Rider is more interested in toxic waste than his repair work," Josh added.

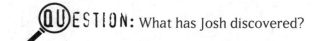 **QUESTION:** What has Josh discovered?

CLUE EIGHT: Moving

Josh saw a can of poison, with a skull and crossbones, just in front of an oil barrel.

The detectives called Tony and explained the situation to him. Tony assembled a team to follow the suspect.

"I'll take over the investigation tomorrow. You can come with me if you'd like," Tony offered.

When school let out the next day, the three friends hurried into Tony's unmarked police car waiting at the curb. They would hide in the car to spy on Don Rider.

The group saw Don Rider move several objects into the courtyard and then toss them into a rented truck. Then he sped off.

Tony tried to follow him, but the car wouldn't start!

"This really isn't the time," he growled, punching numbers on his cell phone. He got through to the police station and gave the dispatcher the license plate number. He also asked for someone to bring him another car as quickly as possible.

Ten minutes later, the detectives were hot on Don Rider's trail. They were lucky, because Don Rider's truck had broken down not too far from his shop.

Tony pulled over. While the police inspector acted like he was conducting a routine search of Rider's truck, the detectives looked through his cargo.

"He's missing something!" David cried.

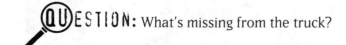 **QUESTION:** What's missing from the truck?

CLUE NINE: New Friends

"There was a tiny white bag in the courtyard, but I don't see it here," David explained to his friends.

"Do you have anything to declare at the border?" Tony asked Don Rider, handing him his papers. Rider seemed like he was on his way to Canada.

"No," he answered grumpily.

"Are you sure?" Tony insisted.

"Absolutely," replied Rider.

"Okay, you can go around," the inspector said, disappointed that Rider didn't slip up and reveal himself.

"That's great, Officer, thank you. But what am I supposed to do about my flat tires?"

Tony didn't respond and hurried to join the others, who were waiting for him in the squad car. They decided to follow Don Rider's route back into town to see if he had really thrown the bag away. They stopped the car several times along the way to search for the bag but had no luck. The bag was small and impossible to spot from a distance.

After the tenth false alarm, they gave up. They pulled over to pet a little pony that was chewing on some grass by the side of the road, while Robinson said hello to two ducks bathing themselves a little farther into the marsh.

"Come on, kids! Back to work!" Tony said after a few minutes had passed.

"No, wait! I think I found the bag that we're looking for!" Lily cried.

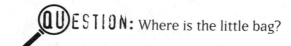 **QUESTION:** Where is the little bag?

CLUE TEN: Mosquito Marsh

Lily noticed the little bag sticking out of a hollow tree stump nearby. Tony put on a pair of rubber gloves and carefully opened the sack. There was a strange yellow powder inside.

"I don't know what this is, but I think it ought to be enough evidence to arrest Don Rider."

Tony brought the bag to the lab for testing. They got results the next day: The powder was a very toxic pesticide.

"I think Don Rider must be a carrier for people who want to get rid of dangerous chemicals as cheaply as possible," Frank guessed after hearing the news.

"What?!" Lily couldn't believe it. "You mean, he gets paid to dump this stuff in the woods?"

"Yes, Lily. At the next town hall meeting, I'm going to ask the mayor to conduct a study on the environmental well-being of the surrounding area."

Two weeks later, the detectives accompanied the scientists on their rounds to study the woods nearby. First, they went to a nature preserve called Mosquito Marsh.

"It's beautiful here," David observed.

"True, but it doesn't stop some people from treating it like a garbage dump," said Josh, disgusted by all the trash he saw.

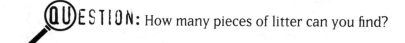 **QUESTION:** How many pieces of litter can you find?

CLUE ELEVEN: One Lie Too Many

Josh counted five things that didn't belong in the nature preserve. He saw a can of oil opened into the water, an open can of paint, a broken bottle, an old bicycle tire, and a crumpled-up tin can.

"I don't know if this is all Don Rider's fault, but I suggest we pay him a visit," said Tony. The detectives said good-bye to the scientists, and all headed over to Don Rider's bike shop.

"You again!" Don groaned when he saw who was at the door. "I'll bet you're not here to get a bike fixed."

"How astute," Tony said. "May we come in? We're here to give you your white sack."

"What sack?"

"Don't play innocent. We know that you get paid to dispose of toxic waste and that you don't do a very good job of it!"

"I have no idea what you're talking about," Rider replied, a little uneasy.

"Oh, really? Then I imagine you also know nothing about a barrel containing a dangerous poison that we found in the river, under the bridge? And I guess you're also ignorant of the fact that the barrel in question had been stolen from Kruger's Root Beer Factory?" Tony said accusingly.

"Kruger's? No, I've never heard of it."

"Don't worry, we've got him," David murmured.

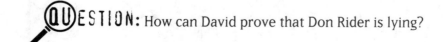 **QUESTION:** How can David prove that Don Rider is lying?

CLUE TWELVE: Birds of a Feather . . .

"How about that?" Tony said after David whispered his discovery in his ear. "Doesn't that belong to you?"

He pointed to Rider's glass, which was sitting on top of a coaster with KRUGER'S ROOT BEER printed on it.

"Fine," Tony continued after Don didn't respond. "The only thing left to do is find out how you got into the factory and managed to steal a barrel of that size."

"I won't say a word until I've spoken to my lawyer," Rider said. Unfortunately for him, a woman walked into the room at that very moment.

"Oh . . . I think I'm interrupting. It's nothing important; I'll just come back later."

"You're not interrupting anything," Tony said, flashing his police badge. "On the contrary. Please, sit down. I have a few questions to ask you."

The detectives quickly learned that the woman was Maggie Dee, the secretary of Kruger's Root Beer Factory and, more importantly, Rider's fiancée.

"You make a lovely couple," said Tony dryly. "But if you'll excuse me, ma'am, I have to arrest your fiancé now." The woman fled the store after Tony pulled out his cuffs.

Tony told the detectives to follow the woman while he dropped Rider off at the police station. Maggie had a bit of a head start, but the detectives found her soon enough. She had disappeared in the community garden.

"Looks like they're the perfect pair," Josh joked. "I know exactly where she's hiding."

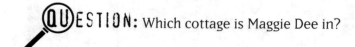 **QUESTION:** Which cottage is Maggie Dee in?

CLUE THIRTEEN: Professional Mistake

"They're perfectly matched, those two!" Lily said. "That's not a garden; that's a dump!"

The detectives tried to sneak into the yard in front of house number 12, but Maggie Dee found them there.

"What are you brats doing here?" she snarled. Maggie was almost as nice as her fiancé.

"We're following you," David said fearlessly. "We know you're involved in all this. We're just waiting for you to confess."

"Oh, yeah? Well, if you're so smart, prove it! Come inside and see if you can find one piece of evidence against me."

The detectives went inside and carefully inspected every inch of the little house. There wasn't really anything of interest inside, and after a while David started to think they would have to admit defeat. The things they found seemed innocent enough: garbage, a few toiletries, and an ugly little garden gnome. They hadn't searched Maggie's basement yet, but what if she refused them entrance? Or worse yet, what if she locked them in? David had just decided to give up when Lily said, "Tell me, Miss Dee, isn't there something strange going on? It seems odd that you would make such a mistake, seeing as you work at a bottling plant . . ."

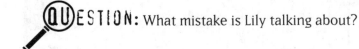 **QUESTION:** What mistake is Lily talking about?

CLUE FOURTEEN: Another One

Maggie Dee's confident expression suddenly faltered. She knew that Lily must have found the root beer barrel on the ground at the back of the cottage.

"That's just a root beer keg," Maggie said innocently.

"Really?" Lily asked. "Do you find it useful to put the tap in the middle of the root beer keg? What do you do when it's almost empty?"

"You kids better get out of here before I get *really* angry!" Maggie Dee cried, leaping out of her chair.

Maggie Dee had a menacing look on her face. She immediately hurried to the back of the house to grab the keg before the detectives did. In her haste, she accidentally knocked the keg over, and out poured hundreds of dollars in cash.

"And there's the polluters' treasure!" Lily announced.

The three detectives quickly fled from Maggie's cottage to call Frank and Tony.

The two men arrived a few minutes later and arrested her.

As Tony was putting the cuffs on Maggie Dee, the detectives noticed a man pacing in front of her cottage. The man ran off once he realized they were watching him.

"That man must be part of the plot, too!" David exclaimed.

"Don't worry," Lily said. "The police will find him. For us, this case is closed."

"How about an ice cream to celebrate?" Josh suggested. Lily and David agreed happily. Best of all, the detectives found the last accomplice on their way to the Ice Cream Palace.

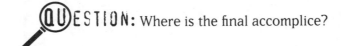 **QUESTION:** Where is the final accomplice?

CLUE ONE: A Storm Brewing

At the police station, Maggie Dee confessed everything. She implicated not only her fiancé, but also the pesticide manufacturer. The detectives had caught the pesticide manufacturer hiding behind a large sign advertising a children's book exposition. His shoes gave him away: They had heels that were two different heights. After Tony questioned him, the man couldn't deny the facts: He had paid Rider a lot of money to dispose of his toxic waste.

The next day, Lily, Josh, and David met up in the afternoon to catch the train to Zimmerville, the biggest town in the next county. The mayor of Zimmerville, Cameron Moss, had invited them to the town's hundred-year anniversary celebration. He had read about Josh, David, and Lily in the paper and wanted to meet the famous detectives.

"I smell rain," Lily said as they left for Zimmerville under heavy gray skies.

She was right. The detectives had just gotten to their rooms at the hotel when an enormous bolt of lightning flashed.

"One, two, three!" Lily counted the seconds between the lightning and the violent boom of thunder that followed. Soon enough, rain started to fall in great, sweeping torrents.

But the following morning, the sky was crystal clear. While the three friends devoured their breakfasts, they heard a radio announcement that said a bolt of lightning had hit the county's police station. At this news, Lily almost jumped out of her chair.

"That's impossible!" she cried. "Come on, let's take a look for ourselves."

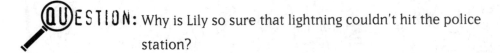 QUESTION: Why is Lily so sure that lightning couldn't hit the police station?

CLUE TWO: Faster Than Lightning

"It's simple," Lily explained to her friends in the taxi on the way to the police station. "There were three seconds between the lightning and the clap of thunder, remember? Light travels much faster than sound."

"Sound waves travel at 1,115 feet per second," David recited. He had studied hard for his most recent physics test. "That means that—"

"The lightning we heard must have hit a point three times 1,115 feet away, which is less than a mile away," Josh continued.

"Exactly. And according to the sign in front of our hotel, the station is one mile away," Lily explained. "Which is why I said there was a problem with that radio broadcast!"

When they arrived at the police station, the detectives learned that the alarm siren had been deliberately disconnected and someone had cut the station's emergency phone cord. And that wasn't all! While the friends were standing in the police chief's office, gathering more evidence, one of the police officers ran up in only his underwear and explained that someone had stolen his uniform!

Suddenly, the phone rang. The police chief picked up and learned that the door to the room containing a display of antique weapons had been forced open and one of the glass cases was broken. Lily, David, and Josh rushed over. It didn't take long to figure out what had been stolen.

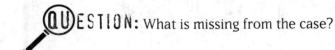 **QUESTION:** What is missing from the case?

CLUE THREE: Letter of (Dis)Approval

The only objects missing from the case were a quiver and its arrows.

"This is an outrage!" the police chief cried. He turned toward his head of security, who looked like he wanted to disappear at that moment like the stolen quiver and arrows.

"How could something like this have happened? No one has access to that room without an official letter of approval. Would you please be so kind as to explain this to me?"

"Here is the letter of approval, sir," the guard replied, shaking a document under his boss's nose.

The police chief quickly glanced over the letter. His face revealed utter bewilderment.

"It's a letter of approval, in perfect order," he murmured. "I can't believe it. If you want to take a look at it, be my guests."

The police chief handed the detectives the letter. It looked very official and even bore the mayor's seal. Leaving the police chief *and* the head of security scratching their heads, the detectives decided to return to the town. If the thief had the nerve to take an officer's uniform and then steal the quiver and arrows right under the guards' noses, he must be bad news. But bad news for whom? The detectives heard the trumpet blast that signaled the beginning of the anniversary celebration sound in the distance. They had decided to go check out the festivities when David suddenly had an idea.

"That's it! I've got it!" he cried. "The letter of approval is a fake! Do you see it?"

 QUESTION: What proved to David that the letter of approval was fake?

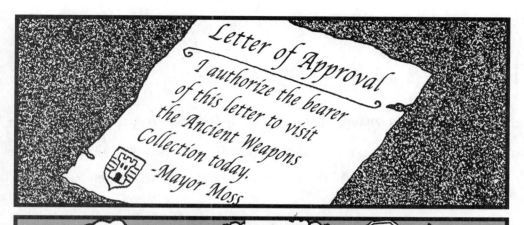

CLUE FOUR: Menacing the Mayor

When the thief made the counterfeit letter of approval, he made an important mistake: Instead of having four crenellations on the top of the tower, the seal on the counterfeit letter had only three! David remembered seeing the same emblem on the flag in the parade.

Mayor Moss was shocked when the detectives met up with him later and told him their story.

"Kids, I feel that it's my duty to inform you of an event that took place quite a long time ago. As you may know, Zimmerville's anniversary celebration has always involved an archery contest between all nine of the major areas in the county. One time, a contestant carrying a black crossbow shot his arrow into a pumpkin. The pumpkin was sitting on the banquet table right in front of the mayor. Unfortunate accident? No. The point of the arrow had been covered in poison. The archer fled the scene. His weapon was locked up in the police station, and his team was forbidden to participate in the archery contest for many, many years.

"Someone informed me that a witness was looking out of his arched window and noticed a man in a hood carrying a black crossbow. I think this new Black Crossbow Archer has ambitions similar to his predecessor's."

The three detectives thanked the mayor for this information and immediately sprinted off to look for the witness. This time, it was Josh who spotted the first clue.

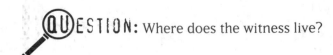 **QUESTION:** Where does the witness live?

CLUE FIVE: Before and After

Josh was proud of himself. Of all the houses on all the streets in all of Zimmerville, only one had an arched window. That was how he knew where the witness lived.

"1768," David read off the stone in front of the house. "This must be one of the oldest houses in the town. What do we do now?"

"There's no question about it," Lily replied. "We go up to the door, ring the bell, introduce ourselves, and hope for the best. Come on, let's go!"

Lily ran up the stairs and looked for the doorbell, but there wasn't one. David and Josh caught up with her and knocked on the door. They knocked once, twice, and then banged on the door as loudly as they could, but no one opened it.

"I guess having good vision doesn't necessarily mean you have good hearing," David said.

"Well, it is possible that he's out," Josh said, pushing the door gently. To everyone's surprise, the door swung open. Josh stuck his head in the doorway and called out loudly. No one answered. The detectives looked at one another, concerned, and then walked into the house, down a long hallway, and up a flight of stairs that led to a huge room with a balcony.

"There's nothing suspicious here," Josh said after glancing around a moment.

"You're wrong, my friend," said David. "Someone escaped us, but just barely. Come on, we can still catch him!"

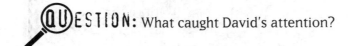 **QUESTION:** What caught David's attention?

CLUE SIX: A Mute Witness

"When we came into the house, someone was here, and it certainly wasn't the witness!" David explained quickly. "Look at the balcony. There were three cacti on the railing when we were outside. Someone must have knocked one off while we were in the hall. Then, while our backs were turned, he snuck out of the house quietly."

"But wouldn't someone have seen him leave the house?" Lily objected. "Unless . . ."

She didn't need to finish her sentence—Josh and David already understood. The three detectives ran down the stairs and pushed open the little door at the end of the hallway that led out onto the garden. A man was lying in the grass, pale and limp. He looked like the owner of the house. Next to him were the cracked remains of a flowerpot, and the uprooted cactus lay several feet away.

"Sir, are you all right?" Josh asked, terrified.

The man didn't respond. David leaned over him, and sighed with relief. The man was still breathing! While the two boys helped the man up, Lily inspected their surroundings. A cat was sitting on the wall of the garden, looking at Robinson with great interest. The cockatoo flew around the yard, screeching unpleasantly. Lily understood right away. Robinson was trying to show her something. He had found a strange object that definitely didn't belong in a garden.

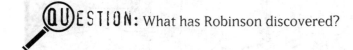 **QUESTION:** What has Robinson discovered?

CLUE SEVEN: Pom-pom

Lily walked up to the rosebush at the back of the garden. Taking care not to prick her fingers, she picked up a ribbon with a pom-pom sewn to both ends. It looked exactly like the ribbons that the security guards wore on their uniforms. The intruder must have lost it as he was fleeing. Had he climbed over the wall or over the iron fence? It wasn't important. Either way, the thief was in excellent shape!

The owner of the house, on the other hand, was not. He started to come to his senses, but couldn't remember anything except the sharp blow to the head that had knocked him out. A neighbor brought the poor man to the hospital, worried that he had a concussion.

The following morning was the first day of the annual festival. The detectives climbed to the top of the town's highest tower. It had a fabulous view of St. Natalie Square, the heart of Zimmerville.

The square was crowded with people. Hundreds of tourists had arrived to see the famous archery contest, which was scheduled for later that afternoon. While they waited for the contest to begin, the tourists strolled through the town and took pictures with the police officers in their uniforms. The detectives were enjoying the view when, all of a sudden, David cried, "Look, it's the fake police officer! This time, he won't escape!"

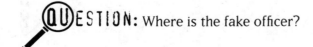 **QUESTION:** Where is the fake officer?

CLUE EIGHT: The Mayor's Enemy

"I don't see him," Josh complained as he furiously wiped off his glasses—a pigeon flying overhead had used them for target practice.

David grabbed Josh's arm and hurried toward the tower's stairs. There wasn't a moment to lose. The fake officer, who was missing one of the ribbons on his pants, was about to disappear under the arch near the house marked number 9. While David, Josh, and Lily struggled through the crowds of people, the man got away.

Unsure of what to do next, the detectives eventually decided to pay a visit to the mayor and tell him what had happened. Even though the mayor seemed preoccupied, he led the kids into his office.

"What a disaster," he said with a sigh, gesturing toward the large stained glass window near his desk. "This glass will be very hard to replace. Before it was broken, the stained glass window depicted the appointment of the very first mayor of Zimmerville. He's the one who was threatened by the poisoned arrow all those years ago. This can't be a coincidence. I think it's some kind of warning. But from whom? To warn me about what? It's a mystery. The thief's silence bothers me the most. If I had gotten one letter or one anonymous phone call, at least I'd know what I've done to make the man so angry!"

"I think you'll know soon enough," Lily said. "Someone has sent you a message."

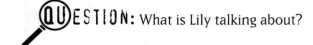 QUESTION: What is Lily talking about?

CLUE NINE: Follow the Arrows!

Mayor Moss couldn't believe it! Behind the glass that protected his antiques collection, Lily had spotted an arrow stuck into the wall, holding a sheet of paper.

With one firm yank, the mayor pulled the arrow out of the wall. He read the message, written in capital letters, aloud to the detectives: "'RETTIRE OR THE NEXT AROW WILL BE FOR YOU!'" A look of horror crossed his face.

"What a disaster!" he cried. "Two spelling mistakes in one sentence! Do you see them, kids?"

Lily, David, and Josh looked at one another, confused. Yes, there should have been only one *t* in *retire*, and *arrow* definitely had two *r*'s, but wasn't the threatening message itself much more important? Turns out, the detectives were mistaken. Mayor Moss explained: "The crossbowman who tried to kill the mayor so many years ago had also warned him by these same means. His message read: 'The Black Crosbow Arrcher curses you and your successors for all time!' Two spelling mistakes in one sentence! Someone wants me to believe in the curse after all these years! It's a bad joke, that's all. Let's just forget it."

But the detectives didn't agree with the mayor. The group decided to take a walk around the center of town.

"If that isn't the famous Black Crossbow Archer," Josh murmured as they walked, "I'll eat my glasses, pigeon droppings and all!"

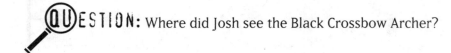 **QUESTION:** Where did Josh see the Black Crossbow Archer?

CLUE TEN: Surprise Attack

The friends ran quickly after the horse and rider that had just disappeared up a flight of stairs at the far side of the square.

Josh was right: The man's quiver, the heavy-duty sack on his back where he kept his arrows, was filled with the same type of arrows they had seen earlier in the mayor's office. The stranger was bold: He hadn't even hidden them!

The detectives ran through the crowd. Every now and then, they hid behind a wall so the man wouldn't spot them. But things got more complicated when the rider left the town limits and started off down a country road. The horse began to trot, then to gallop, and finally disappeared into the countryside at full speed.

When Josh, Lily, and David made it to the edge of the town, all they could see were endless fields and farms stretching out in front of them. David took out his binoculars. He couldn't see anyone.

Suddenly, Josh let out a frantic scream. David dropped his binoculars and turned around to see Josh smacking his pants and yelling, "Help me! They're full of red ants! Ow! That hurts!"

Soon enough, Lily and David were also smacking their pants, trying to fend off attacks from red ants. It took the detectives a good fifteen minutes to get rid of the ants. After another look through his binoculars, David cried—but this time from surprise, not from the biting ants.

"Something's going on at that farm over there," he said. "I think we should check it out."

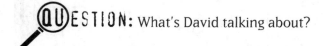 **QUESTION:** What's David talking about?

CLUE ELEVEN: One Queen Down . . .

Who had used the pulley attached to the nearby farmhouse? The pulley's hook was lower than it had been before the ant attack.

The detectives decided to investigate the abandoned farmhouse, and they were glad they did. In the yard, they discovered fresh hoofprints in the mud. The prints indicated that the rider had been there but left in the direction of the forest.

David used a rickety old ladder they had found lying nearby to climb up to the attic. It was filled with all sorts of objects, covered in a thick layer of dust. Then, in the dim light of the attic, David noticed something shiny. It was a golden button from an officer's uniform!

"That must be from the stolen uniform," he announced.

"Yes," Lily said. "But maybe while you're at it, you could explain why the man used the pulley to get up there? That's a little strange, don't you think?"

David had to admit that it *was* strange. But time was running out, and there wasn't a lot of time to think. The Zimmerville festivities had already started! The celebration began with a costume parade: Every neighborhood proudly wore its own colors and carried its flag. Nine elected Zimmerville queens led their neighborhoods in the parade, beaming and waving at all the tourists. The detectives watched the parade from the town walls.

"That's so weird," Lily said suddenly. "I only see eight queens!"

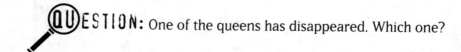 **QUESTION:** One of the queens has disappeared. Which one?

CLUE TWELVE: Queen Laura

"It's the queen of the Flavia district," Lily explained to Josh and David. "I remember her well: She was the youngest and prettiest queen. She was wearing a green taffeta gown with white lace sleeves and sparkly earrings—"

"Okay, Lily," David cut her off. "You're an excellent fashion reporter, but on the crime-solving front, you're a little off. This queen of yours, she's over there—look! She's simply surrounded by her adoring public behind the stone wall. What do you say to that?"

"That I'm going to wait and see what happens," she retorted.

Lily soon learned why the queen of Flavia had disappeared so suddenly. Her name was Laura Oaks, and as she was parading through the streets of Zimmerville, she saw the Black Crossbow Archer. She was afraid and immediately fled to the arms of her beloved father. Nearby, the archery contest was taking place.

"Who won?" Lily asked her friends. She had been distracted by the princess's sudden "disappearance."

"Look at the arrows in the target and you'll find out," Josh told her.

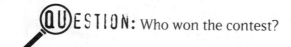 **QUESTION:** Who won the contest?

CLUE THIRTEEN: Target Practice

The man whose arrows matched the one sticking in the center of the target was crossing behind the big tree in the town square. The man had slipped away to prepare himself to shake the mayor's hand and receive his trophy after the celebratory banquet.

The entire population of Zimmerville started to drift toward where the ceremony was taking place. Trumpets blared proudly as the master of ceremonies rose to recite a poem.

"'Long live Zimmerville, our sweet home—'"

But the mayor stopped his poem abruptly. A shrill whistle had sounded, followed by a loud bang. The crowd cried out in shock at the noise and immediately looked toward the mayor, who was terrified. There was a sinister black arrow sticking out of the ceremonial pumpkin!

"That arrow came so close to hitting the mayor!" David exclaimed. "It missed him by a few inches."

"Do you think someone wants to kill him?" Josh asked, suddenly very afraid.

"It looks like it. Someone definitely wants to scare him, at the very least."

"It's pretty obvious to me," Lily said, "that arrow is the sign of the Black Crossbow Archer!"

Josh retraced the arrow's flight with his eyes and discovered where the archer was hiding.

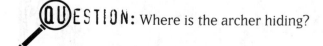 **QUESTION:** Where is the archer hiding?

CLUE FOURTEEN: Masked Mayhem

A crossbow was sticking out from underneath the canvas covering of a horse-drawn cart passing the stone city walls. Josh had noticed it because the cart was moving oddly.

"This time, we've got him. He's cornered," Josh murmured. "David, alert the police. Lily and I will follow the cart."

Lily and Josh hurried after the cart and caught up to it only a few minutes later. But at the exact moment that Lily and Josh were about to step in front of the cart to confront the archer, a man leaped from the cart, dressed head-to-toe in black and wearing a mask. The masked man took off toward the center of town. Josh and Lily were rejoined by David and a few police officers, and together, they all sprinted after the archer.

Unfortunately for the detectives, the masked man had a big head start. When the group reached St. Gavin Square, where the Medieval Market was taking place, Lily was disappointed to discover that they had lost the man.

"It can't be true! He's escaped again."

It was true. While the detectives fought through the crowds of costumed civilians, the Crossbow Archer used the opportunity to disappear. Where had he gone? Just as the detectives were about to call off the search, David cried, "Come quick! I know where he went!"

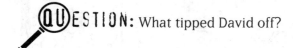 **QUESTION:** What tipped David off?

CLUE FIFTEEN: It's Like a Movie!

David saw the Crossbow Archer's black mask lying on the ground near the knight riding on horseback. The archer must have disguised himself as a knight to escape on horseback!

The detectives nearly caught up with the man as he was turning the corner onto Fountain Square.

But when the detectives arrived at the same place they had seen the man moments ago, the man had disappeared!

"But . . . I don't believe it . . . How could he have gotten away?" the head officer was baffled. "He couldn't have flown away, and there's no way he could have possibly climbed over the city's walls this fast. There must be a rational explanation!"

The detectives and the officers searched the square, but it was useless—the man had disappeared. The officers knocked on the doors of nearby houses, but no one answered. Everyone was at the festival!

"The only explanation is that he climbed through a secret passage in the wall," Lily said.

"You're crazy, Lily! What do you think this is, a movie?!" Josh said. "It's more likely that the marble lions on this fountain ate him!"

But Lily knew she was on to something. After examining the wall closely, she noticed the faint outline of a door in the stone.

"Congratulations, Lily! You were right about the secret passageway," David said. "And lucky for us, I know how to open it."

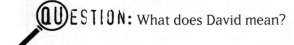 **QUESTION:** What does David mean?

CLUE SIXTEEN: Between Stalactites and Stalagmites

Josh had no idea how right he was about the lions on the fountain. But David suddenly remembered a small detail that had struck him when they first got to the square. One lion's head was tilted ninety degrees when they arrived, but now it was in the same position as the others. *That* must *be the key to the mystery*, David thought happily. *The head on the fountain must control the mechanism that opens the secret door, and another mechanism on the other side must close it*, he decided. To see if his guess was correct, David grabbed the heavy marble lion head with both hands and cried, "Open sesame!"

To his surprise, the head pivoted easily. Seconds later, a slab of rock slid over and revealed the entrance to the secret passageway.

The tunnel was dark, so the group approached it cautiously. Josh went in first, followed by Lily and David. David had turned on his flashlight to guide the way. Inside the tunnel, they found a ramp nestled between low-hanging stalactites that led them deep underground. This was a strange sight, but not as strange as the house that had been built on stilts in the middle of an underground lake! At the bottom of the ramp, a rickety bridge led them over the lake and to the house.

"Be careful, everyone: This bridge shakes!" Josh warned his friends after almost falling off the bridge and into the murky water.

On the other side of the lake, the group looked around the exterior of the house. The only door was locked, and all of the shutters were tightly latched.

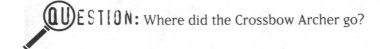 **QUESTION:** Where did the Crossbow Archer go?

CLUE SEVENTEEN: Achoo!

In 1724, a crossbow archer dressed all in black put a curse on the mayor of Zimmerville: The curse condemned him to a lifetime of nonstop sneezing. Since then, the Curse of the Crossbow Archer had been known as the Scourge of Zimmerville. But thanks to a timely twist of fate, the archer's plan backfired, and the mayor got his revenge.

The detectives heard an enormous sneeze erupt in the underground cave. The sneeze echoed, repeatedly bouncing off the cave's walls. The sneeze was immediately followed by the sound of teeth chattering. The Black Crossbow Archer's hiding spot was giving him chills: It was the underground lake!

The archer was clinging to one of the stilts and offered no resistance when the officers picked him up and cuffed him. The archer was just glad that the officers had arrived when they did: The archer might be a great escape artist, but he couldn't swim!

Lily, Josh, and David happily accepted Mayor Moss's congratulations. He awarded the detectives Zimmerville's prestigious Medal of Honor. On the medal's pale blue background was a shiny golden pumpkin, surrounded by palms. Case closed . . . but for how long before a new one appears?